Start-Off Stories

THE UGLY LITTLE DUCK

By Patricia and Fredrick McKissack

Illustrated by Peggy Perry Anderson

Prepared under the direction of Robert Hillerich, Ph.D.

CHILDRENS PRESS ®

CHICAGO

Library of Congress Cataloging in Publication Data

McKissack, Pat, 1944—
  The ugly little duck.

  (Start-off stories)
  Summary: An easy-to-read retelling of the fairy tale
in which an ugly duckling spends an unhappy year
ostracized by other animals before he grows into a
beautiful swan.
  [1. Fairy tales] I. McKissack, Fredrick. II. Title.
III. Series.
PZ8.M458Ug 1986   [E]   85-31428
ISBN 0-516-03982-2

One...two...three
little ducks.

The first little duck is yellow.
The next little duck is yellow, too.

The last little duck
is not like them.

"Oh, you are just
an Ugly Little Duck,"
they say.

One little duck
comes to the water.
Splash!

Another little duck
comes to the water.
Splash!

8

The last little duck
comes to the water.
PLOP!

9

"Oh, you are just
an Ugly Little Duck,"
they say.

10

One...two...three
little ducks in the water.

"I want to play,"
says the Ugly Little Duck.

"No. No. No."

"You are not beautiful like us."

13

"No," says the Ugly Little Duck.
"I am not beautiful like you."

One...two...three
little ducks in the water.

People come.
"Look," they say.
"That duck is beautiful.
"Look," they say.
"That duck is beautiful, too."

"But," they all say,
"that last one is
an ugly little duck!"

18

The Ugly Little Duck
is not happy.

"I will go away," she says.
And, she does.

Fall comes.
Winter comes.

The Ugly Little Duck
is not happy.

Then it is time
to go to the water again.
One little duck
comes to the water.
Splash!

Another little duck
comes to the water.
Splash!

The Ugly Little Duck goes
into the water, too.

"Who is that?"
"Who are you?"

"Who me?
I am the Ugly
Little Duck."

"No No. You are not ugly."
"You are not a duck."

"Oh. Is that me?"

People come to the water again.

"Look," some say.

"That duck is beautiful."

Others say,

"That duck is beautiful, too."

But, they all say,
"Look. Look.
That swan is the most
beautiful of all!"

a	first	no	them
again	go	not	then
all	goes	of	they
am	happy	oh	three
an	I	one	time
and	in	others	to
another	into	people	too
are	is	play	two
away	it	plop	ugly
beautiful	just	say	us
but	last	says	want
come	like	she	water
comes	little	some	who
does	look	splash	will
duck	me	swan	winter
ducks	most	that	yellow
fall	next	the	you

The vocabulary of *The Ugly Little Duck* correlates with the following word lists: Dolch 80%, Hillerich 78%, Durr 76%.

About the Authors

Patricia and Fredrick McKissack are freelance writers, editors, and teachers of writing. They are the owners of All-Writing Services, located in Clayton, Missouri. Since 1975, the McKissacks have published numerous magazine articles and stories for juvenile and adult readers. They also have conducted educational and editorial workshops throughout the country. The McKissacks and their three teenage sons live in a large remodeled inner-city home in St. Louis.

About the Artist

Peggy Perry Anderson lives in Broken Arrow, Oklahoma. She was graduated from Tulsa University with a Bachelor of Fine Arts degree. She is presently employed as an artist at a design studio in Tulsa, where she works on illustrations, ads, and monthly magazines. Peggy and her husband, Kurt, have one son, Brandon. Peggy's interests include writing stories, painting,
and playing the guitar.